KAREN #1 Bestselling Author
KINGSBURY

We Believe in Christmas

ILLUSTRATED BY DANIEL BROWN

ZONDERVAN.com/
AUTHORTRACKER
follow your favorite authors

Donald, my forever love
Kelsey, my bright sunshine
Tyler, my favorite song
Sean, my smiley boy
Josh, my gentle giant
EJ, my chosen one
Austin, my miracle child
And to God Almighty, who has—for now—blessed me with these

K.K.

Bailey,
Forever, may all your Christmas dreams come true.
Papa

We Believe in Christmas
Copyright © 2008 by Karen Kingsbury
Illustrations © 2008 by Daniel Brown

Requests for information should be addressed to:
Grand Rapids, Michigan 49530

Library of Congress Cataloging-in-Publication Data

Kingsbury, Karen.
    We believe in Christmas / by Karen Kingsbury ; illustrated by Daniel Brown.
       p. cm.
    Summary: The joy and sacrifice of the first Christmas is contrasted with the busy and secular holiday season of the present time.
    ISBN-13: 978-0-310-71212-1 (jacketed hardcover)
    ISBN-10: 0-310-71212-2 (jacketed hardcover)
    [1. Christmas--Fiction. 2. Stories in rhyme.]   I. Brown, Dan, 1949-
       , ill. II. Title.
PZ8.3.K6145 Weaf 2008
[E]--dc22

All Scripture quotations unless otherwise noted are taken from the Holy Bible: New International Version®. NIV®. Copyright © 1973, 1978, 1984 by International Bible Society. Used by permission of Zondervan. All rights reserved.

Published in association with the literary agency of Alive Communications, Inc., 7680 Goddard Street, Suite 200, Colorado Springs, CO 80920, www.alivecommunications.com.

Zonderkidz is a trademark of Zondervan.

Printed in China

2006017517   08 09 10 11 • 5 4 3 2

We believe in Christmas and the message of the star.
We believe in Christmastime whatever age you are.
And so let's look for Christmas now; it might be very near—
as close as finding Jesus Christ in what we see and hear.

Then when we talk of wondrous awe,
no matter what we see,
let's think back in wondrous awe, and
there will Christmas be.

And if we speak of readiness and wrappings red and green,
imagine getting ready then, and there will Christmas be.

And when we sing of silent night, and some notes are off-key,
picture that true Silent Night, and there will Christmas be.

When "happy holidays" rings out,
    however real it seems,
remember that first Holy Day,
    and there will Christmas be.

If asking for the perfect gift,
that special thing you need,
think of that one Greatest Gift,
and there will Christmas be.

And should they whisper "I believe…"
when sitting on his knee,
whisper, "I believe this more,"
and there will Christmas be.

When there are cries of angels, child,
    calling joyfully,
see those angels shouting out,
    and there will Christmas be.

And if we want the perfect star to shine upon our tree,
look and see that Brightest Star, and there will Christmas be.

Now when we welcome traveling guests, no matter whom we greet,
remember those three traveling guests, and there will Christmas be.

And if they wish us peace on earth
amid December's weeks,
find the greatest Peace on Earth,
and there will Christmas be.

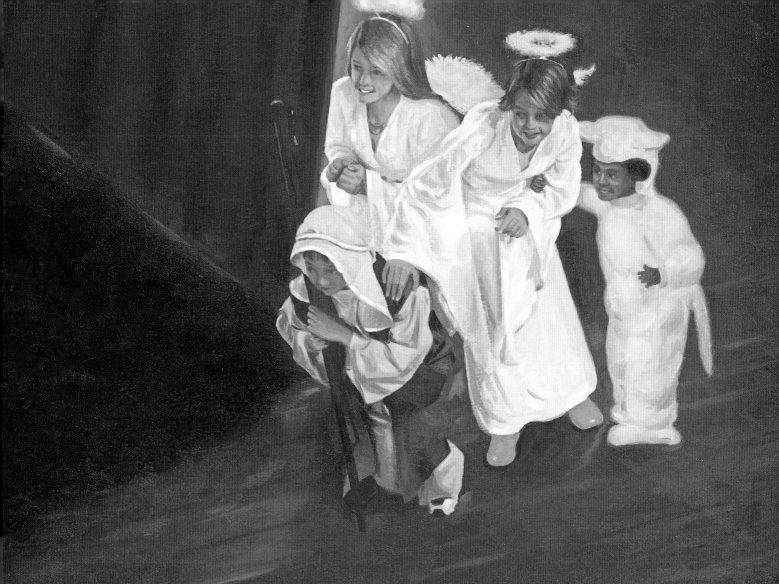

When we gather round the tree,
no matter how much glee,
remember that old rugged tree,
and there will Christmas be.

Yes, we believe in Christmas;
  it's the miracle we need.
When we think of Jesus Christ,
  then there will Christmas be.

For we believe in Christmas, and together you and me will always find our Christmas if it's Jesus that we keep.